JACOB DENNIS FERLAND.
CLASS 1.

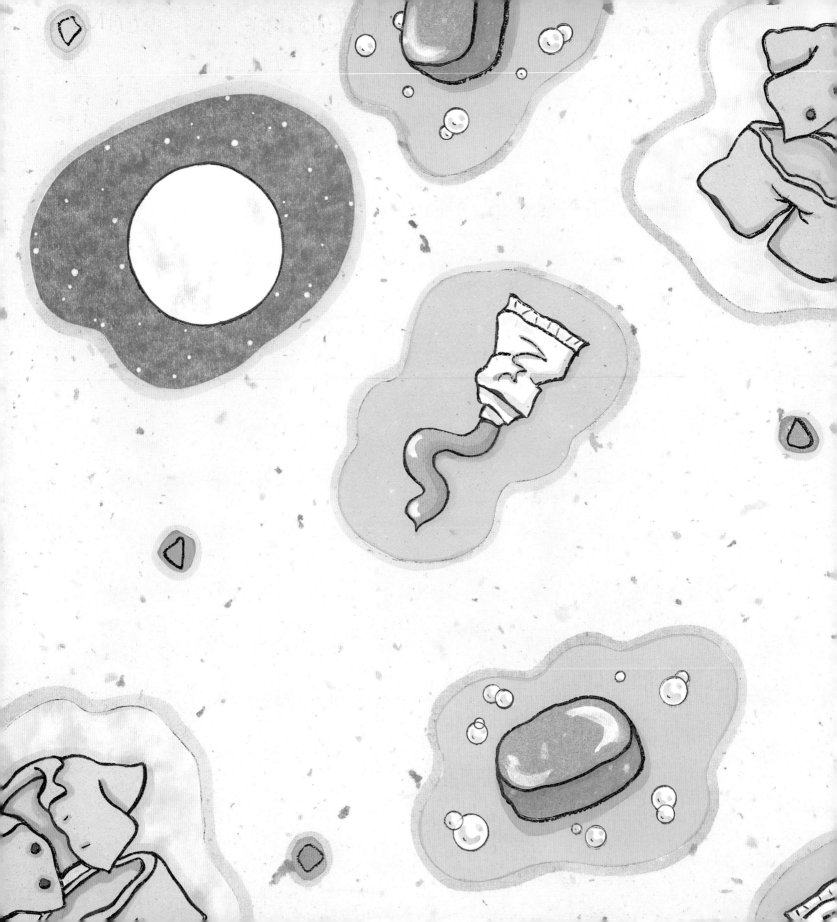

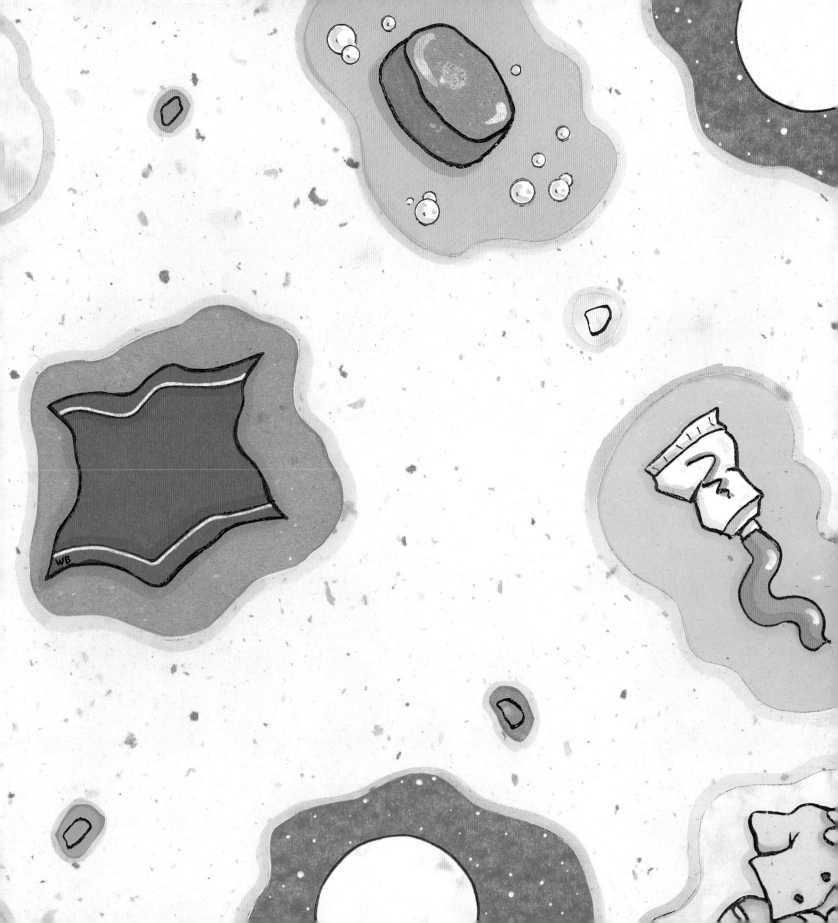

OXFORD
UNIVERSITY PRESS

Great Clarendon Street, Oxford OX2 6DP

Oxford University Press is a department of the University of Oxford.
It furthers the University's objective of excellence in research, scholarship,
and education by publishing worldwide in

Oxford   New York

Auckland   Cape Town   Dar es Salaam   Hong Kong   Karachi
Kuala Lumpur   Madrid   Melbourne   Mexico City   Nairobi
New Delhi   Shanghai   Taipei   Toronto

With offices in

Argentina   Austria   Brazil   Chile   Czech Republic   France   Greece
Guatemala   Hungary   Italy   Japan   Poland   Portugal   Singapore
South Korea   Switzerland   Thailand   Turkey   Ukraine   Vietnam

Oxford is a registered trade mark of Oxford University Press
in the UK and in certain other countries

British Library Cataloguing in Publication Data available

ISBN-13: 978-0-19-279187-0 (Bookstart paperback)
ISBN-10: 0-19-279187-7 (Bookstart paperback)

3 5 7 9 10 8 6 4 2

Printed in China by Imago

Wobble Bear says yellow

IAN WHYBROW AND CAROLINE JAYNE CHURCH

OXFORD

UNIVERSITY PRESS

and this is what she said:

'Now listen to this colour,
try to fix it in your head ~
the colour of this towel is
RED, RED, RED.

Now, what colour is the towel, Wobble?'
And Wobble laughed and he said,

'Yellow!'

Mum took him to the bathroom
and she popped him on the sink.

She said,
    'Look, Wobble,
      this soap is
        PINK!

    Now, what colour
      is the soap, Wobble?'

And Wobble said . . .

'P . . . P .

Then Mum picked up
the toothpaste.
She said, 'Hurry,
Wobble, do!'

Out squeezed a squirt that was BLUE, BLUE, BLUE!

'Now, Wobble Bear.
No mucking about.
What colour toothpaste
did Mummy squeeze out?'
And Wobble smiled . . .
And Wobble said . . .

'Yellow!'

'Right you cheeky Wobble,
I don't want to have a scene.
Put on your nice
pyjamas that are

GREEN,

GREEN,

GREEN!

Now come along, Wobble!
Tell Mummy.
What colour are
your pyjamas?'

And did Wobble say his pyjamas were green?
Nope.

He said . . .
. . . well you know what he said!

Exactly,
he said,

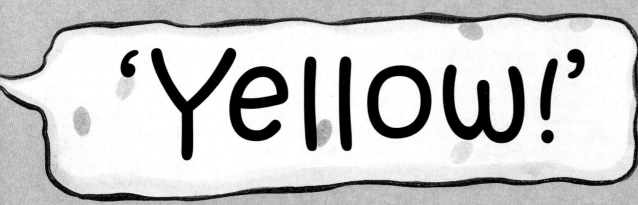
'Yellow!'

Mum said, 'Time for bed,

my funny little fellow.

And take your little teddy

who is really

truly

yellow.'

(Now that was a mistake. She never should have said that
Because Wobble started calling everything yellow.)

He said 'YELLOW' to his dinosaur,

and 'YELLOW' to his pot.

He said 'YELLOW' to his wardrobe,

he said 'YELLOW' to his sheep

He said 'YELLOW' to his welly boots, and 'YELLOW' to his jeep!

So Mum said, 'Yellow is the only word you know

'Just settle down and close your eyes and off to sleep you go!'

So Wobble sucked his thumb a bit,
and gave a little sigh.
And Wobble whispered, 'Yellow'
and he pointed to the sky.

Yes, Wobble whispered, 'Yellow.'
And this time, he was right.
The yellow moon said, 'Clever bear!'
And whispered back . . .
'Goodnight.'

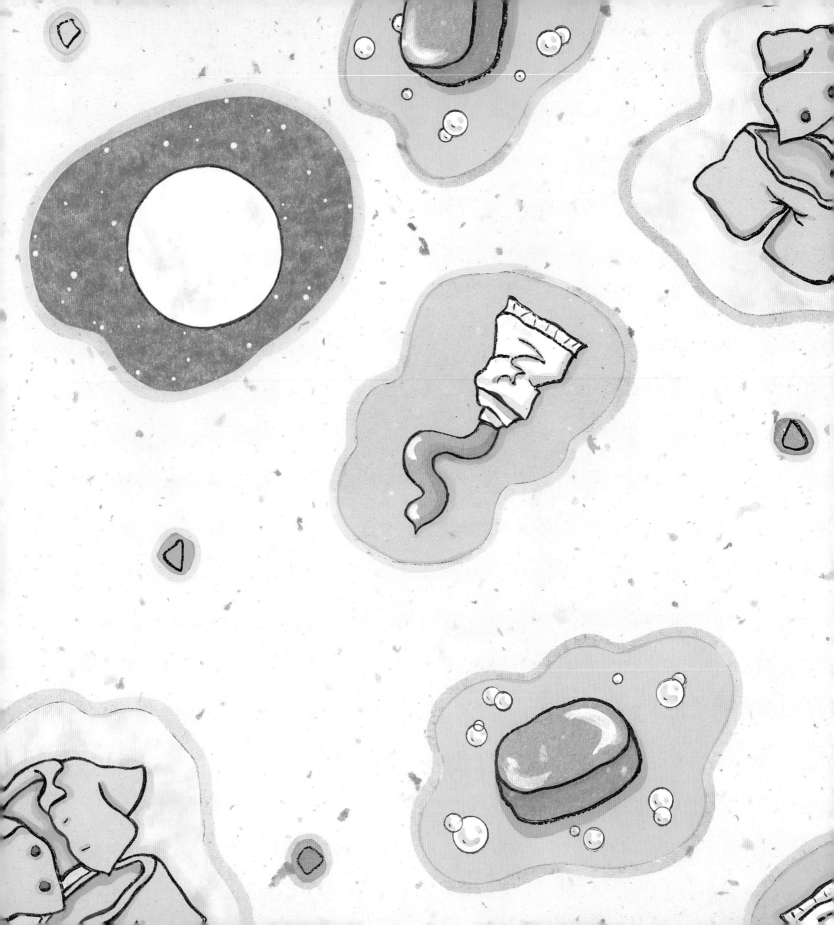

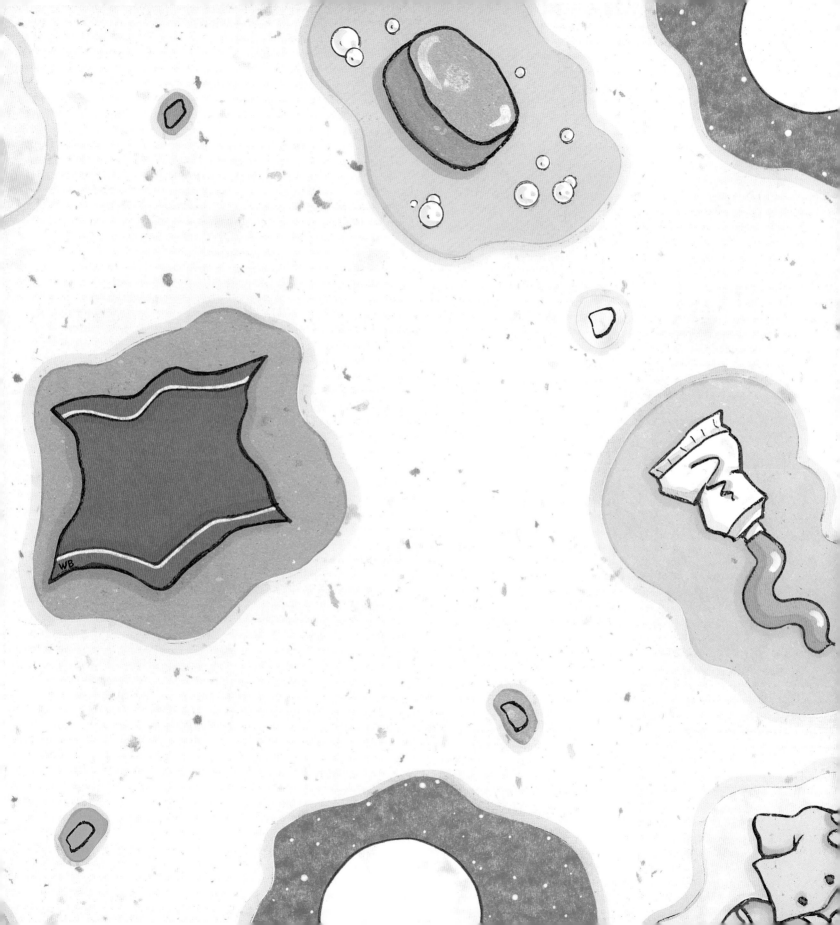